Jimmy Osmond's

AWESOME POSSUM FAMILY BAND

Written by Jimmy Osmond
Character Design by Jimmy Osmond and Bob Ostrom
Illustrations by Bob Ostrom

Regnery Kids

Library of Congress Cataloging-in-Publication Data

Osmond, Jimmy.
  The Awesome Possum Family Band / Jimmy Osmond.
     pages cm
  Summary: When the Awesome Possum Family Band is chosen to perform on
television, the youngest possum tries to find his own special talent.
Based on the life of Jimmy Osmond and his own family band.
  ISBN 978-1-62157-211-4 (hardback)
  [1. Stories in rhyme. 2. Bands (Music)--Fiction. 3. Family life--Fiction.
4. Ability--Fiction. 5. Perseverance (Ethics)--Fiction. 6.
Opossums--Fiction.] I. Title.
  PZ8.3.O8215Aw 2014
  [E]--dc23
                                    2014003306
Published in the United States by
Regnery Kids
An imprint of Regnery Publishing
A Salem Communications Company
300 New Jersey Avenue NW
Washington, DC 20001
www.Regnery.com

Manufactured in the United States of America
10 9 8 7 6 5 4 3 2 1

Books are available in quantity for promotional or premium use.
Write to Director of Special Sales, Regnery Publishing,
300 New Jersey Avenue NW, Washington, DC 20001,
for information on discounts and terms.

Distributed to the trade by
Perseus Distribution
250 West 57th Street
New York, NY 10107

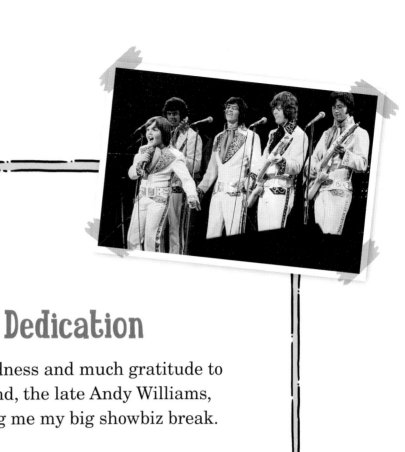

Dedication

With fondness and much gratitude to
my friend, the late Andy Williams,
for giving me my big showbiz break.

 Uh-oh! Who let our hamster Nibbles out!
See if you can find him each time you turn the page.

"Count off," Father Possum called,
one special family night.
All the children gathered 'round.
What an awesome possum sight!

"One" and "Two," "Three," "Four," "Five," "Six."
Then "Seven," "Eight," and "Nine,"
came each reply in harmony.
They sounded oh so fine!

As Father Possum cleared his throat,
he grinned from ear to ear.
Then Mother Possum smiled as well,
and shed a happy tear.

"Your mother has a letter here,
from TV's superstar.
This could be big! Our showbiz break!
And help us go so far."

"Dear Awesome Possum Family Band,
You each are all invited
to star on my big TV show.
We all are so excited!"

You could have heard a pin drop.
Even crickets were so quiet.
Then all at once, they jumped for joy,
and shouted out, "Let's try it!"

The Possums scampered here and there,
each with a job to do.
Except for Possum Number Nine,
who didn't have a clue.

Mother saw him standing there,
so lost and all alone.
She pulled out toys and crayons,
and stayed with him at home.

Aww… "Don't be sad my Number Nine.
Don't worry your little head.
Your talent soon will come to you."
Then she sent him off to bed.

He dreamed and wondered
all the night of things that he could do.
He wanted to feel useful
and help his family too.

One and Two have great jobs,
selling souvenirs at shows.
Posters, photos, albums, too.
"I think I'll have a go."

So off he went the next day,
paper and paints in hand.
Off to make a poster of
the Possum Family Band.

Whoops and oops! Oh, what a mess.
Paint splattered everywhere.
Splashing on the countertop
and even in his hair.

Next he grabbed a hammer, building stage sets with his dad.
Maybe this was where he'd find a talent that he had.

"Come work with me," his father said. "I'll show you what I do."
But Nine got all the wires crossed and the whole place went KAPOO!

"I'm so sorry, Daddy. I really need to go.
I'm running out of time to find my talent for the show."

"Oh Mother dear, please help me
find a spot where I can fit.
Hey, let me make the family food,
and sew costumes for a bit."

Wow! What a mess the kitchen was.
The sewing room—disaster!
A tangled, spangled, sparkly mess!
They both were filled with laughter.

They took a break and went outside, where Mom poured lemonade.
Soon Possum Nine was upside down, resting in the shade.

"It takes some time to figure out just what we love to do.
If you practice, practice, practice, your dreams just might come true."

"What do I love?" said Number Nine.
He took some time to think.
"You'll soon find out," his mother said,
then smiled and gave a wink.

Mother Possum, oh so wise,
she gave him great advice.
"Go practice, practice, practice.
Success comes with a price."

"I know now what I love to do.
I love to sing along."
So he stood outside the window
and sang a brand new song.

He sang, "Oh yeah!" right at the end. His brothers turned around.
They said, "Please do that once again. That was an awesome sound.
It's just what we've been missing. Those high notes can't go wrong.
You're just what we've been looking for to join our family song."

The show began, now almost time
for Number Nine's debut.
A little nervous, still he knew,
he had to make it through!

Father Possum fixed his hair,
said, "Sing with all your heart."
With confidence and mic in hand,
he belted out his part.

"Oh yeah!" he sang, in perfect pitch, to cheers and adulation.
From that day on the Family Band was tops across the nation.

Dear Friends,

I hope you enjoyed my book, *Awesome Possum Family Band*. This story is very near and dear to my heart, as it is based on the true story of the way I grew up.

Yes, I am Number Nine, the youngest member of a pop group/family band called The Osmonds. I started performing with my family on stage at the early age of three. To feel that I was finally a part of the family band was one of the happiest and most exciting days of my life.

Though I grew up thinking every kid did what I did, later in life I realized my life was pretty special. We've been fortunate to perform for a lot of really nice people worldwide (some people call them "fans," I call them "friends"), who have stuck with us through the many years of buying our records and coming to our shows—we couldn't have done it without them. Most of all, I'm grateful to have experienced all of this with a family that I love and loves me.

Over the years, I have had my own hit records and sold-out shows, but I have found it to be most rewarding and fulfilling when I share the stage with my siblings. I have found that when you work for a common goal that helps others as well as yourself, you will find true happiness.

I like being Number Nine!

Jimmy Osmond

Meet the Osmonds
(the Real Awesome Possum Family Band)

Father Possum
George

Stand-up bass and a big booming voice. Our strength, disciplinarian, loving protector, teacher, and guide. After you get past all that—a loving, cuddly teddy bear. We Osmond kids liked to say, "Father might not always be right, but he's still Father."

Mother Possum
Olive

Saxophone and piano. Our loving caregiver, cheerleader, motivator, organizer, sharer of wisdom, and my best friend. Mother was a great cook, loved to collect recipes, and never wasted time. Mother always had her "busy box" with her. It was full of books, scissors, Scriptures, and other projects. Pity the poor Osmond kid who had to carry that very heavy box around for her (and it was usually me)!

Possum #1
Virl

Saxophone and accordion.
Tap dancer, camera buff,
family organizer, publisher,
graphic artist, architect, and
the nicest guy you'll ever meet.

Possum #2
Tom

Saxophone and
piano. Dancer, printer,
photographer, mailman,
fisherman, and friend to all.

Possum #3
Alan

Guitar, piano, and
trumpet. Group leader,
harmony implementer,
songwriter, family
spokesman, and huge fan
of fireworks.

Possum #4
Wayne

Guitar, saxophone, clarinet, flute, fiddle, bagpipes, and many more. Auto mechanic, pilot, inventor, crossword puzzle enthusiast, and family jokester.

Possum #5
Merrill

Bass guitar, trombone, saxophone, and banjo. Songwriter, businessman, scary bear impersonator, and all-around loving, big-hearted guy.

Possum #6
Jay

Drums, saxophone, banjo, and piano. Choreographer, writer, producer, football quarterback, "always there for me" friend and confidant. If ever I have a good day or bad, he's the first one I call.

Possum #7
Donny

Keyboard, saxophone, and
banjo. Electronic genius,
daredevil, best pal who
always got me into trouble,
and Batman to my Robin.

Possum #8
Marie

Guitar and xylophone.
Business entrepreneur,
creative designer,
big-hearted caregiver,
great cook, organizer, and
beloved playmate (even though she liked to dress me up as
her little sister and made me play with her dolls)!
After much therapy, I am okay.

Possum #9
Jimmy

Keyboard, guitar, trumpet,
and congas. First Osmond to
have a hit record (I love to rub
that in), troublemaker, and
the youngest of nine. Can you
imagine the hand-me-downs?

What Is Your Talent?

Hi Friends,

Just like me, you (yes, you!) have special talents too. Maybe you already know what they are. Maybe you are still trying to figure out what they are.

Some talents are really obvious—like my ability to hit the high notes and my brothers' abilities to play musical instruments.

Some talents are not so obvious—like the creative talents of brothers Number One and Number Two.

Sometimes talent shines just by being your most awesome self. Mother Possum was especially good at things like taking care of an entire passel of possums and encouraging worried little possums like me.

So, what's your talent? Your answers to these two questions will give you clues for where to start looking!

Your friend,

Possum Number Nine

1)   What is something you do really well?

2)   What is something you'd like to learn to do really well?

Remember Mother Possum's advice…
Practice, practice, practice until your dreams come true.

Your Time to Shine!

Talents get even better when you share them with others!
Draw a picture of you sharing your talent.

Hooray for you!

Special Thanks

I especially thank my wife, Michelle, and our four children: Sophia, Zachary, Arthur, Isabella, and I can't forget our puppy, Mochi.

I also wish to thank all those who helped me put this book together. Jeff Carneal, thank you for being a lifelong friend and believing in me for all of these years. A great big thank you to my friends Diane Lindsey Reeves and Cheryl Barnes for making this book happen for me.